Pink-Paw's Painting

Illustrated by
Andrew McLean

HAPPY CAT BOOKS

Meet the mice who live in Squeak Street

Old Bun lives in Number One.
His piles of gold shine like the sun.

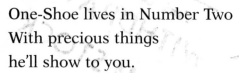

One-Shoe lives in Number Two
With precious things
he'll show to you.

Fee-Fee lives in Number Three
With her enormous family.

Pink-Paw lives in Number Four.
She paints until her paws are sore.

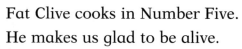

Fat Clive cooks in Number Five.
He makes us glad to be alive.

Quick-Sticks lives in Number Six.
Her band is called the Squeaky Chicks.

Kevin lives in Number Seven.
He thinks old cars
are simply heaven.

Tails the Great, in Number Eight,
Spooks us into an awful state.

Adeline, in Number Nine,
Builds boats — all to her own design.

And post-mouse Ben, in Number Ten,
Is resting his poor feet again.

Published by
Happy Cat Books
An imprint of Catnip Publishing Ltd
14 Greville Street
London EC1N 8SB

First published in Australia 2005 by Working Title Press,
33 Balham Avenue, Kingswood, SA 5062

This edition first published 2007
1 3 5 7 9 10 8 6 4 2

A CIP catalogue record for this book is available
from the British Library

ISBN 978-1-905117-54-3

Printed in Poland

www.catnippublishing.co.uk

Contents

~

Chapter 1
~
Pink-Paw

Pink-Paw was an artist, and she loved to paint. She wasn't rich or famous, but she didn't care. As long as she had paints, food and friends, she was happy.

Pink-Paw made her living by painting cards for the Nice Mice Gift Shop.

But now and then she sold a picture to a mouse who wanted it to hang on the wall at home.

That made her feel like a real artist. It also gave her extra cheese to spend.

She always spent her extra cheese in the same way. First, she went next door to buy a cake from Clive's shop.

Then she rushed to the art shop to buy new paints.

Late one afternoon, Pink-Paw was outside, staring at her door. She liked the big yellow sun she had painted on it, but she felt like a change.

The trouble was that she hadn't sold a picture for a long time. She hadn't been able to buy any new paints. All she had left was black, white, and a tiny bit of blue.

Just then, a shiny red car drove by. The car stopped suddenly and a tall, thin mouse jumped out.

"That door is just what I need!" he said to Pink-Paw. "How much do you want for it?"

"I can't sell you my door!" Pink-Paw exclaimed, very surprised.

"Why not?" said the tall, thin mouse. "You can get another one."

He pulled a cheese bag from his pocket and held it out to Pink-Paw.

Pink-Paw was quite fond of her door. But she needed new paint. And the smells drifting from Clive's cake shop were making her mouth water.

"I wanted a change," she said to herself. "Having no door at all will be a change, for sure."

So she nodded, and took the cheese.

The tall mouse ran back to the car for tools. In a few minutes he had taken off Pink-Paw's door and tied it to the car roof.

"Thank you!" he said. "I'm sure we will meet again."

He winked, got back into the car and drove away, taking Pink-Paw's door with him.

Chapter 2

~

Life Without a Door

Pink-Paw went to buy a cake. Home again, she had just sat down to eat when Old Bun from Number One came by.

"Bless my whiskers!" Old Bun gasped. "Pink-Paw! Your door has been stolen!"

"No," Pink-Paw said, with her mouth full. "I sold it."

Old Bun looked surprised, and went on his way.

Then Tails the Great from Number Eight came along. He was taking his scary pets for a walk.

"Aha!" he said. "Your door has become invisible, Pink-Paw! I will break the spell!"

He took out his magic wand.

"No, no!" cried Pink-Paw in alarm. "My door's not invisible, Tails the Great! I sold it."

Tails put his wand away rather crossly, and walked on.

Next, Fee-Fee from Number Three came in. She had been making green berry jam, and had a jar for Pink-Paw.

"Pink-Paw!" she squealed. "Who broke down your door?"

"No one," said Pink-Paw. "I sold it. Now I can go and buy new paints."

"But you can't go out and leave your house wide open!" said Fee-Fee. "What if a burglar comes? What if Tails the Great's pets get loose?"

She put the jam on the table, and hurried home.

Pink-Paw pushed the last of her cake away. She had decided that life without a door was rather annoying.

"Adeline in Number Nine can make things," she said. "I'll go and ask her to make me a new door. I'll only be away a few minutes. What can happen?"

But while she was gone, quite a few things happened.

First, Ben the post-mouse came with a letter. He tried to knock on the door of Number Four. But there was no door to knock on.

"That's strange," Ben said.

He peered into the house. No one was home. So he put the letter just inside the doorway, and went on.

There was no mail for Number Nine, and Ben didn't stop there. So he didn't see Pink-Paw talking to Adeline.

And he was already at home in Number Ten, resting his feet, when a little breeze blew into Squeak Street.

The breeze found Pink-Paw's open doorway. Just for fun, it picked up her letter and tossed it into a corner. Then it blew the last of the cake onto the floor. Then it got bored, and went away.

Soon after that, some ants came marching along, on their way home from a picnic. As they passed Pink-Paw's house, they smelled the cake.

"Cake! Yum!" they said, all down the line. "Cake-yum-cake-yum-CAKE-YUM!"

They turned and marched into the house.

Chapter 3

~

The Painting

By the time Pink-Paw came home, the ants had finished the cake and were fast asleep under the stove.

Pink-Paw was very tired. She didn't notice that her cake was gone. She didn't see the letter lying in the corner.

She blocked her doorway with a board that Adeline had given her to use until the new door was made. Then she went to bed.

In the middle of the night, she woke up feeling hungry. She got up to have a snack, and saw the letter.

She picked the letter up. On the front it said: URGENT! THE ARTIST, 4 SQUEAK STREET, MOUSEVILLE. Pink-Paw's heart began to beat faster as she read the note inside.

Dear Artist,

The Sunny Corner Home for
Lonely Old Mice opened today.

Our sitting room is nice, but
quite boring. It needs a very big
painting that is interesting and full
of life.

You are invited to bring a
painting to the Home at 9 am
tomorrow. The artist whose painting
is chosen by our judges will get a
very large bag of cheese.

Fergus Fuzz
MANAGER

Pink-Paw looked at the paintings she already had. They were interesting, but not very big. Then she looked at the board blocking her doorway. It was very big indeed.

Pink-Paw's paws began to itch. She wanted to paint that board with all the colours of the rainbow!

But she didn't *have* all the colours of the rainbow. She only had black, white, and a tiny bit of blue. And the All-Night Munchie Market didn't sell paint.

"I'll just have to use what I have," she said. She paced around, thinking.

Then she started work.

It was a long job, but at last the picture was finished. Pink-Paw looked at it while she ate some bread and green berry jam.

At the top was a black bird flying in a blue sky. The bird was looking down at a town of little white houses and winding grey roads.

"The roads make an interesting pattern," said Pink-Paw. "But I *wish* I'd had more colours."

With one finger she smoothed a lump of paint where one road crossed another. The crossing turned green!

In horror, she realised that her paws were covered in green berry jam. She snatched up a rag to wipe the jam off her painting. Then she stopped, staring.

The little patch of green looked good!

Slowly Pink-Paw dabbed some more jam on the road. The road began to look like a path of soft, green grass.

"Yes!" Pink-Paw shouted. She rushed to the table and grabbed the jam jar.

An hour later, all the roads on the painting were a pretty green.

Pink-Paw was very pleased.

When the painting was dry, she pinned a cloth over it, ready for the morning. Then she went back to bed and fell asleep.

But under the stove, the ants were waking up. They stretched, and smelled green berry jam.

"Jam! Yum!" they said. "Jam-yum-jam-yum-JAM-YUM!"

They marched across the floor, and crept under the cloth that covered Pink-Paw's painting.

Chapter 4
~
Sunny Corner

Next morning, Pink-Paw was woken as usual by Fee-Fee calling her many children for breakfast. Quickly she got dressed and ran to ask Kevin in Number Seven to drive her to Sunny Corner in his truck.

Soon they were on their way. Pink-Paw felt very excited.

"There will be lots of artists there," she told Kevin. "It will be hard to park."

But when they reached Sunny Corner, only two artists stood waiting outside the Home for Lonely Old Mice.

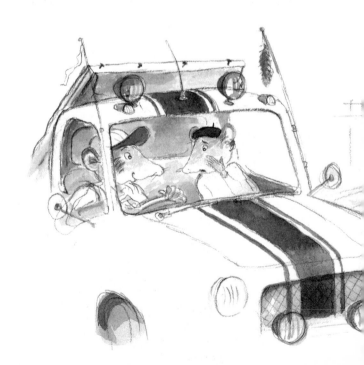

Pink-Paw gasped. The artists were Ava Nibble and Al Fresco, whose pictures were often in the *Mouseville News*.

"Those artists are really famous," she whispered to Kevin.

"So what?" said Kevin. "I'll bet your painting is just as good as theirs."

But Pink-Paw felt cold with panic as she walked up the path. She wasn't famous. Why had *she* been asked to bring a painting? That letter must have been a mistake!

"My dear, isn't this door just too *awful*?" she heard Ava Nibble say to Al Fresco.

"It's *very* yellow," said Al Fresco. "But it's cheerful. And it *does* match the Home's name."

Ava Nibble sniffed.

Pink Paw saw that the door was *her* door — her sun door! Her ears grew hot.

"I don't think we've met," Al Fresco said to her. "Are you from out of town?"

"No," said Pink-Paw. "I'm — um —"

Just at that moment, the door opened. There stood the tall, thin mouse.

"Greetings!" he said. "I am the manager, Fergus Fuzz."

He led them into a large, white room where lots of old mice sat chatting and playing cards.

"Please put your paintings here," said Fergus Fuzz, waving his hand at a bare wall.

Ava Nibble and Al Fresco took the covers off their paintings and leaned them against the wall. The old mice turned to look.

Al Fresco's painting was a very interesting pattern of red and silver triangles.

Ava Nibble had painted what looked like a family of worms that had gone blue with cold.

Pink-Paw's paws trembled as she took her painting's cover off. And when she saw what was underneath, she nearly fainted.

Her painting was crawling with ants!

Chapter 5
~
The Winner

Pink-Paw stood frozen with horror. This was the worst moment of her life.

"Move aside!" snapped Ava Nibble. "No one can see!"

Pink-Paw shut her eyes, and moved. There was a moment's silence. Then suddenly there was a roar of sound.

She opened her eyes, amazed.

All the old mice were clapping and banging their sticks on the ground. They were shouting and cheering.

"Fur and feathers, look at that!" cried Al Fresco. "It's a town of ants! It's Antville!"

Pink-Paw's mouth fell open. She looked at her painting again.

And then she realised that the ants weren't crawling *all over* the painting.

They were running along the paths of green berry jam, stopping now and then to chat or eat.

So the town really *did* look like Antville.

"Well," said Fergus Fuzz, beaming. "It seems we have our winner."

"Rubbish!" snapped Ava Nibble. "The judges will decide who wins!"

"The judges *have* decided," said Fergus Fuzz, waving his hand at the cheering crowd.

"But they're just a bunch of old mice!" Ava Nibble screeched. "They don't know anything about art!"

"No," said Fergus Fuzz. "But they know what they like. And that's all that matters here."

Ava Nibble went red in the face, picked up her painting and left. The old mice cheered even louder.

Fergus Fuzz shook Pink-Paw's paw.

"I'm glad you won," he said. "Your door gave me the idea to buy a painting in the first place."

"How did you train the ants to stay on the roads?" asked Al Fresco.

"Oh, it wasn't hard," said Pink-Paw weakly. "I — "

But just then Fergus Fuzz gave her the very large bag of cheese, and she had to thank him. So she never did tell Al Fresco about the green berry jam. And that was lucky, because Al Fresco often copied other artists' ideas.

As it was, the Sunny Corner Home for Lonely Old Mice was the only place in Mouseville with a painting that was so interesting, and so full of life.

The old mice knew its secret, but they didn't tell. They were very happy. They loved it when Pink-Paw visited them every week to put new jam on the ant paths. So did the ants, who adored their new home.

And Pink-Paw was very happy too. She had lots of new friends. She had lots of extra cheese to spend. And, of course, she had a brand-new door to paint — in every colour of the rainbow.